The Big Yummy Treasure Chest

By
Darshna Morzaria

AuthorHouse™ UK Ltd.
1663 Liberty Drive
Bloomington, IN 47403 USA
www.authorhouse.co.uk
Phone: 0800.197.4150

Yah pustak Shri Gokulotsavji Maharaj aur Shri Thakorji kee krupa se sidh huo raihi hai.

Published by AuthorHouse 9/27/2016

ISBN: 978-1-5246-6378-0 (sc)
ISBN: 978-1-5246-6379-7 (e)

Print information available on the last page.

This book is printed on acid-free paper.

author HOUSE®

Foreword

"A lovely interactive book that shows the relationship between a child and their childminder. Developing healthy eating habits within their Early Years is essential to children's lifelong well-being and it's refreshing to see a book that supports this."

Laura Henry

International Early Years Specialist

LauraHenryConsultancy.com

About Laura

Laura is a leading, award winning expert in Early Years education, both in the UK and internationally. For three decades she has used her skills to support colleagues who work directly with children, parents and companies.

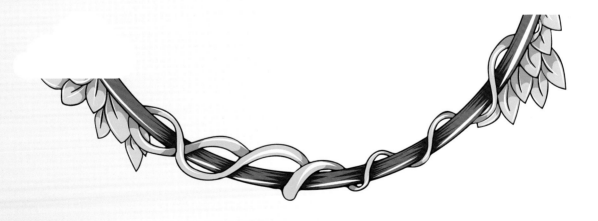

Dedicated to

This book is dedicated to my loving dad, who made countless personal sacrifices so that I would not go without.

He taught me to dream, and then work hard to make those dreams come true.

He inspired me to reach for the stars, and then shine like one in the night sky.

Even though you are not here, you inspire me in everything I do.

About
AUTHOR

Darshna Morzaria is a home-based childminder in Harrow, west London. She has over 20 years' experience of working with children and young people in a variety of roles prior to becoming a childminder.

Although childminding from home, Darshna's setting has facilities more like a nursery. This gives parents confidence that their child is receiving the best of both types of early education – homely and professional.

More recently, Darshna has started to incorporate the Forest School ethos into her setting. This is a great illustration of her passion to keep evolving and improving her skills and qualifications so that she can offer every child she cares for the very best start in life.

In 2016, Darshna was shortlisted as a finalist in the coveted Nursery World Awards.

Website: LittleDarling.co.uk

Twitter: @LittleDarlingHa

FaceBook: Facebook.com/LittleDarlingHarrow

YouTube: YouTube.com/c/LittleDarlingUK

Little Darling Childcare

Finalists
Nursery World
Awards 16

Little Sammy liked playing with mum and dad,
but playing with other children seemed to make him sad.

"All my friends
run faster
than me.

They can jump up high. They can climb a tree."

Little Sammy loved all things sweet,
but fruit was something he wouldn't eat.
"YUCK!"

But his loving childminder changed his mind,
her name was Darshna and she was very kind.

"I'll take little Sammy on a magical trip, he'll love the fresh fruit on my pirate ship."

They made their way through a secret trapdoor,
and looking at the magical pirate ship,
he thought to explore!

Keen to now put things to the test,
Darshna opened a big shiny chest.

Sammy licked his lips
and rubbed his tummy,
the treasure chest of fruit
smelt really YUMMY!

First he picked a pineapple,
a juicy piece to trial,
and soon enough,
his eyes lit up,
and then a great big smile.

Next he chose a mango,
it glistened in the sun,
and soon enough,
it was clear to see,
how quickly he could run.

Now what looked like an apple,
time to give it a chance,
and soon enough,
he started to move,
and found himself doing a dance.

Next he reached for the pear,
he wanted to give it a try,
and soon enough,
he bent his knees,
and jumped up to the sky.

Last was the banana,
He gave it a great big bite,
and soon enough,
he left the ground,
and flew as high as a kite.

The time had come to head home,
and Sammy with his filled tummy,
ran and ran, as fast as a car,
and shouted "FRUIT IS YUMMY!"